Henry Hacon

The Incarnation

And other Poems

Henry Hacon

The Incarnation
And other Poems

ISBN/EAN: 9783337206420

Printed in Europe, USA, Canada, Australia, Japan

Cover: Foto ©Andreas Hilbeck / pixelio.de

More available books at **www.hansebooks.com**

THE INCARNATION

AND OTHER POEMS.

By HENRY HACON,

VICAR OF SEARBY-CUM-OWMBY, LINCOLNSHIRE.

BRIGG :

JACKSON AND SONS.

LONDON :

SIMPKIN, MARSHALL, HAMILTON, KENT & CO., LTD.

1898.

PREFACE.

In 1851 some juvenile verses of mine were published at my native town, Swaffham, in Norfolk. So that it is after a long interval that I am venturing to put forth another book. It contains what I have written during the last year or two.

In the larger poem I have glanced at the mistake of separating the Atonement as a doctrine from the doctrine of the Incarnation; in other words of making the Incarnation simply a necessary prelude to the Atonement instead of accepting the Incarnation as that great counsel of the Eternal God (of which the Atonement is a part), the climax of which is to be the conversion of the world and the union of its races into one holy temple on the two foundation stones, which that Incarnation has blended into one, of the Fatherhood of God and the Brotherhood of Man. How far I have succeeded in giving expression to this truth must be left to the verdict of the reader. Both of this poem and of the shorter ones that follow, I would say in the motto of an old English bard:

Candide, si mala sint nostra inter carmina, parce ;
Et bona si quæ sint, Zoile, parco tibi.

Searby Vicarage,
September 12, 1898.

TO MY NATIVE TOWN.

Rigid Utility's unsparing hand
Hath fenced in all the commons of the land.
And so thy wild heath, Swaffham, now no more
Sweeps round thee as it did in days of yore.
There oft I wandered in that happy time
When first my thoughts did wed themselves to
        rhyme.
And now, impelled by that sweet memory,
I dedicate these later lays to thee.

CONTENTS.

THE INCARNATION.

SWIFTER than the light of morning travels from
    its central source
Angel-messengers from Heaven were speeding
    on their earthward course ;
And as spirit speaks with spirit in a tongue to
    man unknown
Was the wondrous consummation of a hidden pur-
    pose shewn ;
And the Great Eternal Presence boundless as
    the boundless space,
Seemed at one mysterious moment to assume
    that winning grace
Which is seen when worldly greatness stooping
    from its station high
Draws from hearts a holier homage by its meek
    humility.
E'en as when some high-born mortal gives his
    hands to servile toil,
Easing in his weary day-task a poor brother of
    the soil.
For at that mysterious moment, where the resting
    cattle fed,

B

One became a feeble infant in a Bethlehem
    stable-shed :

He the Son, the Wellbelovëd, Second of the
    Primal Three,

In the Bosom of the Father resting from
    eternity,

Coming in His lowly greatness from a stainless
    Virgin's womb

For a life of daily labour and a humble cottage
    home.

In the world of art and nature searching eye
    could never see

Aught that gives a worthy image of that awful
    mystery :

Yet from art and nature's garden human thought
    may dare to cull,

As she treads its winding mazes drinking in the
    beautiful,

Here and there a fragrant blossom which her
    hand may fitly twine

For a wreath where richer offerings blaze before
    His lowly shrine.

Think we then, in lordly Athens how great
    Pheidias of old

Bodied forth his spirit's vision in the ivory and
    the gold :

Thus by Spirit-wrought conception in that Beth-
    lehem stable lay
Essence Uncreate Eternal coupled with soul-
    quickened clay.
For by power more than Pheidian in Redemp-
    tion's gracious plan,
Not a false god but the True God deified the
    form of man.
Look too where in cloudless ether night's meek
    maiden mounting higher
Draws a superadded splendour from some planet's
    silver fire :
So it was when Heaven's Daystar sheltered from
    earth's rude alarms
Lay in infant weakness folded in the Virgin-
    mother's arms.
For the star that adds the splendour, though so
    small to mortal sight,
In its glory and its vastness soars above the
    satellite.
Thus it was that the Great Presence circling
    heaven and earth and sea
Gave a sign that mortal man was One with His
    Infinity.
And the angels caught the signal, and, revealed
    in glory bright,

Told the tidings to the shepherds watching o'er
　　their flock by night.
Oh the wonder, oh the glory, oh the benefit
　　unpriced,
Of the Hypostatic Union in the Person of the
　　Christ!
Sitteth He that lowly craftsman heir of want and
　　woe and pain
Where the angels at His glory veil their eyes
　　with pinions twain;
And the God whose word of power ruleth heaven
　　and earth and hell,
Sits a worn and weary wanderer asking water at
　　the well.

Mortal man whose soul hath followed science in
　　her wondrous flight,
Tracing all her starry progress through the
　　watches of the night,
Let thy knowledge teach thee wisdom: how
　　much really dost thou know
Of the common things around thee in thy brief
　　life here below?
Evermore is science baffled: all her triumphs
　　seem to teach

That beyond them lieth mystery which no human
 quest can reach.
Climb to mental heights no other mortal man
 hath ever trod :
Then fall down and kiss the shadow of the
 mystery of God !

Seemeth it a thing that passes all belief that He
 whose word
The deaf void of non-existence in obedient
 silence heard,
Bursting into germs of being for development
 sublime,
Æon merging into æon in the onward lapse of
 time,
Should forego His Godhead's greatness, and,
 enwrapped in swaddling bands,
Take a poor and lowly portion with the creatures
 of His hands ?
Go we then in humble pondering to the revelation
 high
Which declares the searchless mystery of the Holy
 Trinity.
Never must we in that doctrine fail the difference
 to see

Twixt the One Eternal Essence and the Per-
    sonality.

Life inherent hath the Father, life that could be
    given by none ;

And to have that life inherent He hath given to
    the Son.

And the Eternal Son from heaven was sent to do
    the Father's will ;

And His meat and drink was ever that great
    purpose to fulfil.

In that Triune Life Eternal Perfect without void
    or flaw

Thus we see in mystic dimness meek subordi-
    nation's law.

So an earthly son and father both a common
    nature own ;

But the son's subordination by the very name is
    shown.

Thus it is that God's sweet order man's rude
    violence doth leaven ;

For the things of earth are shadows of the higher
    things in heaven.

Vain to ask : " Could God's free mercy fettered be
    to such a plan ? "

Rather mark the demonstration of His wondrous
    love to man ;

And, as fruit of that example, how in many a soul
    of worth
Godlike love can quell and conquer all the blan-
    dishments of earth;
Where a man, for mission-labour to reclaim a
    world undone
In a deadly sphere of duty, doth not spare his only
    son ;
Or where one in youth's fresh vigour, drawn by
    love's resistless spell,
Gives himself to holy labour where the loathly
    lepers dwell.
And the gate is closed upon him till he draws his
    latest breath
Poisoned by the fell contagion of that brotherhood
    of death.
Look again what shades incongruous form the
    texture of man's life,
Order with disorder mingling in a never-ending
    strife.
In him is a noble instinct that doth urge him to
    aspire
Evermore and evermore to something deeper,
    broader, higher,
Ever altering or destroying that which he hath but
    begun,

Following hope that beckons onward till a farther
    goal is won.
But the range of active working mortal man can
    compass here
At its best is all too narrow for his soul's sublime
    career.
Plans and projects stand unfinished when his
    working days have sped,
Like the shattered shaft that mourneth over the
    untimely dead.

Heaven's sweet boons of love and friendship seem
    precarious gifts of chance,
Resting, flitting, gleaming, fading, like the wild-
    fire's fitful dance.
Many mutually fitted to combine in concord sweet
Live and die in lonely longing, for they never
    chance to meet.
And though of a full expansion every sign the bud
    may show,
Death or change or chance may wither the fair
    flower ere it blow.
For a little boy and maiden come with spirits free
    and wild
For a summer morning's pastime with a solitary
    child.

What are all the acquisitions to which older hearts
    are glued
To his joy that summer morning in his sylvan
    solitude,
As he points out all the wonders of the hill-side
    and the plain,
Sits with them upon the green grass, lengthening
    a daisy-chain,
And within his infant bosom feels the first delicious
    thrill
Of that heaven-born affection which alone the heart
    can fill ?
But those bright, fresh hours of sweetest soul-
    communion quickly fly,
And the joyous summer shouting changeth to a
    sad good-bye.
And he stands in speechless sorrow, and his tears
    begin to flow,
Watching them as through the meadows hand in
    hand they homeward go.
Other things will stir his bosom, other things will
    fill his day ;
Fairy forms of sunbright fancies stay their wings
    with him to play.
But at times o'er his young spirit comes a boding
    sense of pain,

As, with pensive brow, he thinketh : " Will they
    ever come again?"
No, my child; for fever's blighting power hath
    their pathway crossed ;
And thy playmates of an hour are among the
    loved and lost.
Through the stages, as they follow, of his ever-
    changing life,
He may meet with much to cheer him in the
    world's conflicting strife :
Comrade-schoolmates' arms thrown round him,
    mutual secrets heard and told,
Sympathies of heart more precious than the miser's
    hoarded gold ;
Gentle hands to smooth his pillow when his
    temples throb with pain ;
Words of love and power that make his fainting
    spirit strong again—
But through all the lights and shadows of a long
    life's chequered round
Love and friendship in their fulness never never
    hath he found.
And a gray-haired man is sitting by his solitary
    hearth,
Weighing heaven's unseen completeness with the
    emptiness of earth.

World-distractions once so potent now no more
    his soul can move;
And his heart is sad within him, pining for a little
    love.
And his thoughts are going backward to that
    happy summer day
When the little boy and maiden joined him in his
    merry play,
Back to the green grassy meadows where they
    wove their daisy-chain;
And once more he asks the question : "Will they
    ever come again?"

Yes, how soon the bright tints vanish of our child-
    hood's early morn;
And the shadows deepen o'er us as we near our
    destined bourne.
Still that joy, though all the dewy freshness of its
    prime hath fled,
Giveth now and then a token that it is not wholly
    dead.
There's a sphere of thought and feeling known
    to us and God alone,
Where we hear the mystic music of the child-life
    that is gone ;

And it acts upon the spirit like the wind-harp's
    whispering string,
Or the sweet and subtile odour of the early blooms
    of spring.
But the din that rises ever from the world's un-
    resting throng
Drowns the soothing intonation of its murmurous
    undersong.

Would'st thou then in faith and patience grasp a
    truth that can assuage
All the woe and weary languor of thine earthly
    pilgrimage,
Ponder thou the wondrous doctrine on which hangs
    the gracious plan
Of fallen man's regeneration : " Man is God and
    God is Man."
Twixt the sinful woe-worn mortal and the God he
    cannot reach
Lo the mighty Daysman standeth, and a pierced
    hand toucheth each.
And by virtue of that contact man a perfect life
    can win,
Where his heart shall faint no longer 'neath the
    weary stress of sin,

Grasping the full compensation of that glorious
    new birth,

Reading all the hopeless riddles which perplexed
    him here on earth,

Finding friendships which had withered green
    again, as Aaron's rod

Burst forth into bloom and fruitage 'neath the
    quickening power of God,

Free from death's foreboding shadow, free from
    every care and pain,

The glad joy-bells of his childhood ringing in his
    heart again.

All too feeble is our earthly embryo vision to
    descry

What thou art and what thou art not, fathomless
    eternity !

Strive we how we may to rise up into thy sublime
    idea,

Still we people thee with forms that are familiar
    to us here.

Boundless space—within whose vastness all the
    rolling spheres of light,

All the suns whose scintillations gem the dusky
    brow of night,

Are but as the tiny midges of the sultry summer
    day,
That in inter-twining orbits spin their little lives
    away—
Gives no solid consolation to the restless soul of
    man,
Claims no kindred with the heart-joys of his being's
    earthly span.
Speculation speaketh to him : " Mortal, let thy
    spirit's eye
Pierce the cloud that veils the mystery of thine
    unseen destiny.
Up on higher scales of being thou shalt mount
    for evermore,
Every dawning acquisition richer than the one
    before :
Unknown powers of spirit-rapture, unknown
    powers of force and will ;
Objects in succession endless all those faculties
    to fill.
Ay, 'twere well if we could bring ourselves by
    exercise intense
To a pillared saint's abstraction from the things
    of time and sense.
But our soul mid the conditions of a finite life
    like this

Droops and faints beneath the heavy burden of so
    vast a bliss.

We would fain imagine something less
    oppressively sublime,

Some restored and sinless pattern of this life of
    sense and time.

Use hath mighty power o'er us : here our sen-
    tient life begun ;

In their grooves our habits circle like the planets
    round the sun.

Though his heart can dance no longer to the
    ringing chords of mirth,

Yet man clings with fond persistence to his
    heritage of earth.

Fair and sweet as infant-dreamings spring hath
    flown on rainbow wings ;

Summer hours have passed for ever with the
    warmth that summer brings ;

Autumn of its teeming fruitage gave a rich and
    full supply ;

Scant and withered are the relics that within the
    garner lie.

But the man, though sitting sad and silent in his
    wintered home,

Croucheth o'er life's dying embers till his sleeping-
    time is come.

Thus although we feel assured it is better to
    depart,
Yet the old life-long conditions keep their hold
    upon the heart,
And though how 'twill be we know not, yet we
    trust that there will be
A revival of our earth-joys in the great
    eternity.
And He who came to dwell among us, Head and
    Saviour of our race,
Showeth that the two conditions may
    harmoniously embrace.
Though He spoke in solemn warning of the awful
    doom of sin ;
Though He taught us we must bravely fight if we
    a crown would win ;
Though He tells us we must sternly pluck out the
    offending eye,
Cut the hand off that would draw us from the
    paths of sanctity ;
Yet He shared in man's rejoicings where the
    marriage-feast was spread,
Groaned in spirit with the mourners who were
    weeping for their dead;
And He shews us the poor wanderer to his
    father's love restored,

Once more in a son's apparel sitting at his father's
　　board ;
And the music and the dancing filled the hall with
　　festive sound
For the dead son that was living and the lost one
　　that was found.
And our life in all the fulness of its sympathy
　　and love
He hath joined in endless union to the perfect
　　life above.
Thus the overpowering grandeur of the life that
　　is to be
Softens neath the homelike colours of the things
　　which here we see.
So, while all the valley round me laughed in
　　summer light below,
Have I seen the Himalayas in their everlasting
　　snow.
There they stand, those mighty landmarks, planted
　　by the Hand of God ;
There upstretch the icy passes ne'er by human
　　footstep trod ;
Bulge the buttresses tremendous from yon bul-
　　wark's frowning wall,
Where the stern unbroken silence doth the very
　　heart appal.

With a gaze of silent rapture we that distant
  scene behold;
Yet we seem to shiver in us: for it looks so
  deadly cold.
But the sun that o'er the earth's wide circuit
  spreads his golden light,
In his occidental glory sinking slowly from our
  sight,
Over yonder glittering home of snow a gorgeous
  mantle throws,
Tinging all its marble grandeur with the colour
  of the rose.

Sinner, in thy chainless freewill thou hast played
  an evil part,
And the guilt of thy transgression lieth heavy on
  thine heart.
Rules of wise and holy living taught thee when
  thy years were young
In the ripening of thy manhood's folly to the
  winds were flung.
Thus, with faltering steps deserting wisdom's
  straight and narrow way,
Thou did'st try some smoother bypath lured by
  pleasure's Siren lay.

But not long thy footsteps falter : crowned with
    riot's drooping flowers,
Thou art blindly, madly, wasting all thy young
    life's golden hours.
And although thy palate sickens, there's a hand
    that doth supply
For thy pall'd inebriation cups of deadlier
    potency.
Deeper, darker, grows thy ruin; to the dog
    whose dinning tongue
Fills thee with forebodings drear an atheistic sop
    is flung :
" They are fools and blind who credit all that
    men have fondly said
Of a great unseen Creator who shall judge the
    quick and dead.
'Tis the weary repetition of an old and worn out
    song
Which the policy of priestcraft through the ages
    doth prolong,
Cheating us with specious shadows of imaginary
    good,
Offering empty cups and platters in exchange for
    solid food.
For man cometh as the brute comes, and his
    functions are the same ;

And he dieth as the brute dies, and is but an
    empty name."
But though thus thou hast departed from thy
    Maker, yet doth He
Of His love and tender mercy still retain a hold
    on thee,
Through the midnight silence speaking in a voice
    with terror rife,
E'en as when the thunder crashes o'er a levin-
    blasted life ;
And thy dormant conscience, wakened from its
    slumber by that voice,
Owns the depth of thy transgression, owns the
    folly of thy choice.
Far worse than the moral doubter in thine error
    thou hast been :
His fault is a vicious judgment ; thou hast bartered
    faith for sin.
Know thou surely atheistic thought, so far from
    being free,
Is for man the direst, bitterest, soul-enshackling
    slavery.
If thou ask why demonstration is not open to
    thine eye,
In thine own self-conscious being thou can'st read
    a full reply.

Think of all thy body's functions : thou would'st
    never say, I ween,
That in walking, running, leaping, 'twas a self-
    impelled machine.
Art thou not thyself the will whose impulse all
    that motion sways,
And whose faintest hint the body simultaneously
    obeys ?
Can'st thou frame a mental mirror where the
    features of that will
Backward thrown upon themselves a perfect
    semblance shall fulfill ?
Would'st thou then the true existence of thy
    conscious self deny
Because no form of it is focussed in the circle of
    thine eye ?
What else therefore is it, only in a richer, higher,
    way,
The great universe around thee working without
    stint or stay,
Stretching on, and ever onward, in its grand and
    cosmic plan
Farther far than thy weak sight with all its optic
    helps can scan,
Elements together mingling from whose action
    swift or slow

Issue forms of complex beauty human workshops
    cannot show ?
Plain it is then, though He be impervious to our
    human sense,
There must be a great Propelling Personal
    Omnipotence.
Yes, the reasons that have led thee thy Creator
    to deny
Stand on worse grounds than the grounds of
    sceptical philosophy.
God was a restraint upon thee in thy passions'
    evil day :
Thou would'st crush it into nothing, sweep the
    bugbear clean away.
Now at length of thy transgression thou dost taste
    the bitter part,
And the vulture retribution feeds upon thy living
    heart.
But no Titan-courage in thee, with a sullen sense
    of wrong,
Steels thee in thy spirit's bitter dole " to suffer
    and be strong."
And thy life upholds thee only to endure thy
    misery,
Like the plank that bears the shipwrecked sailor
    up upon the sea.

And the sky is brass above him, and the wave is
    liquid fire ;
And the eyes of hungry monsters follow him with
    fell desire ;
And he drifteth till night's darkness adds its
    horror to his doom :
O'er the lonesome waste of waters now no human
    help can come.
Thou would'st fain shake off the terror, and
    forgiving mercy clasp,
And tear thyself once and for ever from thy
    sorrow's clinging grasp ;
And thou criest from the dark and dismal depth
    of thy despair :
" Is there any balm in Gilead ? Is there a
    physician there ? "
For between thee and thy Maker stands a wall of
    triple brass,
Through whose folds thy fainting spirit struggles
    all in vain to pass.

But at length a healing power o'er thy sickness
    seems to move ;
And the song of the creation is once more the
    voice of love.

Now to taste of purer pleasure ; now from what
    God made so good
To supply thy spirit's healthy craving with its
    proper food.
Ocean's briny breeze shall check the creeping
    growth of languor's pain,
And bring the rosy flush of health back to thy
    pallid cheek again.
Free from carking care's distraction, thou shalt
    rove from clime to clime,
Where thy fertile fancy revelled in the day-dreams
    of thy prime.
Fairest scenes of earth shall charm thee with an
    ever-new delight ;
Cities of renown shall open all their treasures to
    thy sight.
Ah, poor mortal, trusting this way permanent
    repose to win !
Thou art blind to the insidious power of formulated
    sin :
For as when in some hidden hollow of the mine
    a vapour stays,
To strike terror by its ghost-like murmur after
    many days :
So can sin, by this or that diversion for awhile
    kept under,

Uplift its cruel sword again and cleave the very
    soul asunder.
Tis as if the boaconstrictor should relax his dire
    embrace,
For an antepast of false hope in his helpless
    victim's face.
There is that can charm the serpent, and his deadly
    folds shall be
Weak as are the trustful twinings of the arms of
    infancy.
But thou yet must learn a lesson deeper, if not
    bitterer, far,
Of how vain without thy Maker all thy best
    endeavours are.

In thy desultory wanderings thou hast come to
    mighty Rome,
Once the Old World's stately palace, now its
    grand memorial tomb.
By an interest unflagging day by day thy feet are
    led
To the ruined homes and hauntings of the great
    historic dead.
Thou art standing in the Forum, and the stones
    beneath thy feet

Are of those that Horace trod on near the
cloistered Vestals' seat,
When the opportune subpœna gave the courtly
poet rest
From the intolerable babbling of his pertinacious
pest.
From the lower excavations now thou wendest to
the hill
Where the lives of trembling courtiers hung upon
a tyrant's will,
And thy keen imagination revels in its strength
among
Those crumbling walls which still ring back the
echoes of satiric song :
Here, Rome's lords, in due obedience to the
imperial behest,
Sat in grave deliberation how the turbot should
be dressed ;
There, still shines the tessellated pavement of
the banquet-room
Where, in purple-cushioned ease reclining,
favoured guests had come ;
And the eyes of Cæsar gloated when he saw the
monstrous fish
All but overlap the spreading margin of the
Samian dish.

But ere half thine explorations are completed thou
  dost feel
The shadow of a weary languor o'er thy sated
  spirit steal.
But change of scene can still stave off that creep-
  ing horror's deadly hold,
Like fresh fuel on the fire that keeps the tiger
  from the fold.
So from land to land thou rovest like the legen-
  dary Jew,
After dead enjoyment ever seeking something
  strange and new.
Thus, not finding what thou lackest in fresh
  places, thou art come
Again to wander mid the stately ruins of imperial
  Rome.
And thou triest to be happy: but in vain : for joy
  is free
And forceless as the glinting light that dances on
  the summer sea.
Now a sudden recollection moves thy fancy to
  explore
The Tabularium's gloomy chambers ; for when
  thou wert there before
Thou wast near a hidden danger from an un-
  fenced stair beneath ;

And, stumbling at it in the darkness, thou
    might'st well have met thy death.
Now upon the wall beside a little oil-lamp's
    friendly glow
Breaks the thick gloom and warns the traveller
    of the treacherous depth below.
" Ah, since then" thou thinkest "some one must
    have death or damage found,"
While I, escaping such disaster, stand here once
    more safe and sound.
Is it merely chance that brings me to this self-
    same spot to-day ?
Rather, is it not a voice from God, inviting me
    to pray ?
Surely His love was waiting till in union com-
    plete
Conditions tending to my spirit's permanent
    repose should meet."
And thou lookest up to heaven for remission of
    thy sin,
And for grace to cleanse thine heart from every
    stain that lurks within.
And a loving presence round thee seems to scatter
    all thy fears,
Bringing back the careless calm and buoyant hope
    of earlier years ;

And thou criest in a welcome sense of rest from
    weary strife ;
" Oh be this my joyful birthday to a new and
    better life ! "
And, as if in gratulation of thy soul's release,
    there swells
Through the vault's imprisoned gloom a mingled
    peal of sweet church bells.
For it is the Eve of Easter when Rome's streets
    and lanes along
Sounds the silver-chiming prelude of her resurrec-
    tion-song.
As when one who loves to wander where the
    spring with lavish hand
Scattereth her boons of beauty o'er the winter-
    wasted land,
Sees the young buds of the hawthorn, sweetest
    flower of sweet Maytime,
Drooping 'neath the untimely rigour of the
    blossom-blighting rime :
But the sun beats back the spoiler, and the flower
    clothes the thorn,
To cheer the hearts of early workers at the open-
    ing of the morn ;
And the breeze conveys its fragrant summons to
    the wandering bee

To gather while the Maytime lasteth from those
    blossoms plenteously :
Thus, while those sweet bells are ringing out their
    holy Easter chime,
Thy sorrow-blighted zest of life awaketh to its
    early prime.
So thy rovings thou renewest with a lightsome
    heart again,
Deeming thyself free for ever from thy spirit's
    heavy chain ;
And mid the whirl of busy cities, o'er the sweep
    of dales and dells,
Soundeth still the soothing echo of those happy
    Easter bells.
But how sweet soever earthly echoes sound in
    marble domes,
At length through graduated waves of mellow
    murmuring silence comes.
Thus what seemed a prayer-won boon thy sorrow-
    wasted soul to bless,
Though thou strivest to retain it, echo-like grows
    less and less ;
Till of all that golden sunlight every lingering
    trace is gone,
And again thy world-worn heart is left to pine its
    woe alone ;

And the dread recurring burden of thy weariness
    and grief
Presses on thee all the heavier for that respite
    bright and brief.
And while sorrow's bitter portion seems to quench
    all happier choice,
A still more terrible temptation utters its seductive
    voice :
"If there be a God who made thee, why when
    thou hast fairly tried
To secure thy soul's contentment, with religion for
    thy guide,
Should He mock a heart that trusts Him with a
    vain and specious show
Of peace that bideth for a season but to aggravate
    thy woe ?
Give the fruitless struggle over ! What more can
    religion do ?
Wilt thou court its tantalizing visions all thy brief
    life through ?
Fair and full has been the trial thou hast made of
    the control
Of strict and self-restraining rules upon the im-
    pulse of thy soul.
It has failed thee : bow thy neck to superstition's
    yoke no more :

And thy grasp on life's enjoyments will be firmer
 than before."

But there's a voice, if man will listen, which will
 drown the Siren's breath
That, in dulcet measure flowing, lures him to the
 shores of death ;
And that voice with power persuasive speaketh to
 thine inner ear ;
And, still craving for relief, thou bowest down thy
 soul to hear—

Mortal, when the voice of conscience called thee to
 amend thy ways,
And to give to wisdom's guidance all the remnant
 of thy days,
Far too shallow was thy turning : just a light con-
 fession said,
A mere whitewash of repentance o'er thy black
 transgression spread ;
Then in milder joy to seek a refuge from the sore
 distress
Which justly upon hearts to sin enslaved is ever
 wont to press,

Mingling with it such sufficient measure of religious
  leaven
As should zest thine earthly portion with the
  happy hope of heaven.
Did'st thou think by such a penance God's absolv-
  ing grace to win ?
Was it ought but an addition to thine unrepented
  sin ?

But that hour when from thy sadness thou did'st
  gain a glad release,
And Mercy seemed to meet thy prayer with all
  the fulness of its peace ;
And, iridescent with the light of heaven from
  feeling's deepest wells,
The fountain of thy joy leaped up responsive to
  those Easter bells :
Was it but a fond delusion ? was it but a devil's
  lie?
And if in truth it was from God, oh why did it so
  quickly fly ?
Nay : for as the good God maketh suns to rise
  and showers to fall,
Bringing harvest's genial blessings as a common
  boon for all :

D

So, sounds that strike upon the ear and sights
    that fill the wond'ring ken,
Can join in combination sweet to witch the willing
    souls of men.
There's a touch of subtile power even in insensate
    things,
Which to sorrow-burdened breasts a present con-
    solation brings.
For, in weariness of life beneath some deep heart-
    hidden woe,
One hath courted soothing slumber when the
    summer sun is low.
Head upon his hand he sleepeth in oblivion of
    his pain,
Living for a little moment in the happy past
    again,
In some scene of life's brief morning all unstained
    by sorrow's tears,
Looming in the shadowy dream-land through the
    mists of bygone years.
And he wakes up from his slumber as the dying
    daylight falls
In a shower of golden glory o'er the relics on the
    walls ;
And the odours through the window streaming
    from the garden's bloom

Blend mysteriously with those vision-shadows of
    his childhood's home.
So by memory's magic music melancholy's ghost
    is laid ;
As from Saul the evil spirit passed away when
    David played.
But where was all the disenthrallment of his harp's
    melodious spell,
When the gloom of Endor's cavern bickered with
    the fires of hell ?

But thou thinkest : " If the soothing charm I found
    in beauty's quest,
Which, a sweet reaction bringing, gave my weary
    spirit rest,
By the inevitable doom of all things earthly took
    its flight,
Why should my religion cheat me like a vision of
    the night ?"
Ah, but was it such religion as sustains the droop-
    ing heart,
Not mid favoured spots of nature, not mid
    miracles of art,
Not where an o'erflowing coffer drains the pam-
    pered fancy dry,

Not where health embrowns the cheek and flashes
    from the laughing eye ;
But where within the choking mine or mid
    machinery's deafening play
A dull routine of weary toil employs the hands
    from day to day ;
Or where some sudden crushing loss has bowed
    the rich man's honoured head,
And straitened means can scarce supply the
    humbler home with daily bread ;
Or where the sick man hopes no more his former
    vigour to regain ;
For, drop by drop, his life is slowly ebbing out in
    sleepless pain ?
Yes, there's the risk for those whose cup with
    earthly good is brimming over,
A snare which in our hours of joy is not so easy
    to discover,
That self-indulgence unrestrained will grow at
    length to such excess
As, with its fatal swamping might all heart-religion
    to suppress.
E'en as the bird that soars and sings is made
    dumb by the muttering thunder ;
Or as a death-grip from below can drag the
    strongest swimmer under.

And such a feeble thing as that avails thee
　　nothing in the hour
When hell, back-beaten for a time, renews the
　　assault with deadlier power.
For they alone can know, who feel the writhings
　　of the worm within,
How strong and clinging is the grasp upon the
　　heart of cherished sin.
The band which fluttered loose at first, so slight
　　and silky-soft, at length,
Almost before we're well aware, has bound us
　　with a cable's strength.
Ah, of the words of weary woe which from sin-
　　burdened hearts arise,
As if in a despairing wail, up to the pure and
　　pitying skies,
Oh none are sadder sure than that which cryeth :
　　" Oh I would be good,
I would be wise, I would be true, I would be
　　holy, if I could !"
When all the healthy joys and cares of life
　　sufficing man before,
Blighted and withered by his sin, can feed his
　　pining soul no more ;
And, powerless as a little child within a giant's
　　sinewy arm,

All the whole soul is drawn within the focus of
    some damning charm.
Alas, poor soul! no woe of earth can be compared
    with woe like this:
Its gloom is pointed with a flame that cometh
    from the black abyss.
So was it when, in dalliance fond with tempting
    words, Eve's eye was made
To fix its glance upon the fair and fatal fruit
    which God forbade.
The beauty and the bloom were gone from all
    that charmed her wiser hours :
There was no splendour in the sky, no music in
    the leafy bowers ;
And all the fruits so fair and good which God had
    given so full and free,
Were soured and blackened by the blight which
    breathed from that forbidden tree.

But there's that which, apprehended rightly, can
    in truth supply
With heaven's own food the pining famine of thy
    weary misery.
For God the Eternal Son, who dwelleth in the
    high and holy place,

Took into Himself a mortal nature to redeem
    our race.
Mystery of love stupendous, deeper far than
    thought can gauge !
Learn its sorrow-soothing lesson ! Read it in the
    sacred page !
Not in the imperfect version some with good
    intent have given,
Narrowing in their earthly blindness that which
    came complete from heaven,
Enforcing duly the Atonement for our sins by
    Jesus made ;
But leaving all the rest of Incarnation's doctrine
    in the shade.
For, to gain the strength and comfort that great
    doctrine can supply,
We must see it in the light of its divine
    philosophy.
Divine : for it pervades the truth that was to
    holy seers revealed,
And stands for ever in the scroll by God's own
    Spirit signed and sealed.
And all the teachers of the word who in their
    prudent steps have trod,
Have used it as a mighty means to win the souls
    of men to God.

Do we hold that evolution is the great creative
    law ?
Then, in reverent contemplation, we may this
    conclusion draw :
Step by step from form minutest a life-giving
    power expands
'Till man, the flower of the creation, in his Maker's
    image stands.
But, God's holy law transgressing, he hath fallen
    from his height,
In his body soul and spirit smitten with a
    deadly blight ;
And the whole creation groaneth, waiting for a
    glad new birth
From the clinging curse transmitted by the fallen
    lord of earth.
Thus there needed a remaking : so shall the
    corroded chain
Link by link in pristine beauty glad the eyes of
    God again ;
And the sin-defaced creation be in light and love
    restored
By the renovating virtue flowing from the Incar-
    nate Lord.
Thus that wondrous Incarnation crowneth
    evolution's plan ;

And in Jesus Son of Mary we behold the perfect
    Man.

And we see a law of contact in the realm of heart
    and mind,

By which the feeble can grow strong, the foolish
    wise, the coarse refined.

So has one of nature's princes in the olden times
    gone by,

Dowered with an angel's heart and dowered with
    a prophet's eye,

Sought and found prevailing power to uplift a
    prostrate race ;

And he comes down from the mountain with God's
    light upon his face ;

And in prudent legislation gives them rules they
    can obey ;

And by words of suasive wisdom wakes the
    soul within the clay.

And in every age are prophets faithful to their
    holy trust,

Whose burning words have power to raise our
    grovelling spirits from the dust.

Thus in wondrous condescension taking human
    flesh and soul,

God the Son, the Pure and Holy, came in
    contact with the foul :

That man the child of sin and sorrow, maimed in
    heart and maimed in limb,
Might be raised and cleansed and healed in mystic
    union with Him.
He can free thee from the bitter anguish of thine
    evil hour,
And lift a holy hand to touch thy leprous soul
    with healing power.
Tempted : He can succour those whose souls are
    by temptation torn ;
Once Himself a child of sorrow, He can feel for
    those who mourn.

As a member of the Body of the God-Man, claim
    thy place
In the glad regeneration of the covenant of
    grace.
This hath been the double burden weighing on
    thy soul within,
A sickening sense of ill-desert, the power of thy
    besetting sin.
But the perfect absolution that doth from His
    passion flow   ·
Can purge thee from thy guilt and make thee
    whiter than the driven snow ;

And the miserable thralldom that hath held thine
    heart so long
Can in Him be crushed and broken, who is
    stronger than the strong.

And though temptation, still recurring, should thy
    feeble heart assail,
Cling to Him in firm persistence ; and in Him thou
    shalt prevail.
Dreary still may be the valley where thy fainting
    footsteps tread ;
And the burning blast of noon may beat upon
    thine aching head ;
And, from out the straight path lying, shady
    groves may woo thee still
Of their God-forbidden solace to enjoy thy
    wonted fill.
Stay not ! Turn not ! Look not ! Think not !
    firmly fix thy faltering eye
Where, like clouds, in the dim distance yonder
    spreading uplands lie !
Bravely bear thy spirit's anguish, treading o'er
    that treacherous ground ;
Like the savage who has pierced his quivering
    flesh with ghastly wound,

And hangs in torturing impalement till his
    straining fibres part,
Drinking fortitude's stern lesson into his
    barbarian heart—

Thou hast gained the height at last where all
    God's faithful ones have stood;
And the bracing breeze of heaven is pouring
    health into thy blood;
And farther onward, through the mists that for
    awhile must round it cling,
Thine eye can catch a distant glimmer of the city
    of the King.

THEN AND NOW.

One summer's morn—'twas in my boyhood's
  prime—
  I lay reclined within a woodland dell,
Listening in spirit to the silent chime
  That Zephyr ringeth on the heather-bell.
Within me, like a deep sea's rippling swell
  Dyed in the cloudless heaven's empurpling
  blue,
The wavelets of my young thoughts rose and
  fell—
  Thoughts that were then so beautiful and true—
Tinged by that Light from heaven which maketh
  all things new.

And fifty changeful years have come and gone;
  And, mid the flowering heather once again,
I listen to the bell, with solemn tone
  That tolls its measured knell from yonder fane,
Telling how youth's full-orbëd bliss must wane,
  And all its splendour merge in formless gloom,
Melting in tears like frostwork from the pane,
  Until there seems 'neath fate's remorseless doom

No balm save kindly death, no refuge but the
    tomb.

In winter's frost we pine for flowery spring :
    It comes, but bringeth not the wished-for joy ;
And time o'er every hard-won gain doth fling
    The brooding shadow of some heart's annoy ;
The bright hopes cheat the man, which cheered
    the boy ;
And the heart droops neath sin's sirocco blast ;
The fine gold changeth into base alloy ;
    And dead eyes with heart-crushing kindness cast
A sad, reproachful gaze out of the tideless past.

But hark, a still voice speaks : "O grovelling soul,
    Stint not thy view to time's o'ershadowing
      night !
Through yon blue depths where myriad systems
    roll
If thou could'st speed thee with an arrow's flight
The infinite would mock thy feeble might.
    Thy life is there, thy home, thy native clime ;
Thought cannot gauge the rapture of the sight."
    I listened—and the darkness changed to light ;
And the heath-bell once more rang out its matin
    chime.

A VANISHED FACE.

In the aurora of our life's brief morn,
   Ere labour's stern exactions claim our hands,
When the young heart by care is all unworn,
   Blessing and blessed some gentle woman
     stands,

In human form acting an angel's part,
   Mingling her soul in childhood's smiles and
     tears,
The magic of whose manner wins the heart,
   And keeps her memory green through all the
     years.

Whether she's dead or only old and gray
   We know not: for we see her now no more ;
And yet on us her sweet face shines alway
   In all the freshness of the days of yore.

Such things pass from us : the relentless law
   Which severs hearts its course unswerving
     runs :
We see not now the sights which once we saw ;
   And we change ever with the changing suns.

We miss the fulness of the love which blessed
   Our earlier years ; and we are fondly fain
To find where it abides : it mocks our quest ;
   And the search ends in disappointment's pain.

Whether it be on land or over seas
   The seeking and acquist are far asunder ;
As echo only answered Hercules
   When pearl-wreathed arms drew shrinking
   Hylas under.

THE VOICE OF THE CREATION.

I groan in travail-throes of complex pain
  From Heaven to Earth, from Earth to Sheol
    below
'Till one strong word shall break obstruction's
    chain
  And ease my pangs and let the burden go.

Wherever man acts his allotted part
  Evil with good and foul with fair is crossed ;
And in the secret shrine of every heart
  Lingers a saddening sense of something lost.

Earth's homes are full of weary souls that pine :
  Sweet hopes have fled and left them all forlorn :
Hopes bright and brief as when the orient brine
  Laughs back the golden kisses of the morn.

Look where through mad ambition's selfish quest
  Man meets his brother man in deadly strife !
Look where drought closes the Great Mother's
    breast,
  And plague and murrain blast the breath of
    life !

Nor is the burden only borne below :
  It stirs heaven's bliss with ripplings vague and
    dim :
A shadow falleth on the golden glow,
  A sadness on the songs of Seraphim.

As the blood curdles with a sudden chill
  Caught from some troubled spirit wandering by,
In some gay group when pipe and tabor thrill
  Their souls with music's winsome witchery;

Or as a child amid her birthday glee
  Feels her young heart with heaviness oppress'd
To find the little birds she comes to see
  Gasping and dying in their frozen nest:

So those good spirits sigh in pity wide
  As they look downward from their home above:
E'en as when He looked up to heaven and
    sighed,
  The Great God-Man amid His works of love.

But as when life stirring the void beneath
  In dædal beauty from night's troubled womb,
Burst into form beneath the Quickening Breath :
  So will it be when my birth-hour is come.

Then when the awful recreative nod
  Shaketh time's chaos through its depth and
    height
The joy song of the morning-stars of God
  Shall thunder through the corridors of light.

THE VOICE OF THE ANGEL.

As one who, standing on a grassy mound,
Drinks in the woodland melodies of morn :
So stand I on this whirling globe of earth,
And listen, as the myriad-circling spheres
Roll their sweet thunder through the fields of
    space.
Yet, in a power by God to us transferred,
We can conform to human thoughts and acts.
As once with Abraham talked the Mystic Three,
And rested on their way, and ate man's food.
And now I go to one whose wavering youth
Hath yielded to temptation, and the snake
Hath wound his first coil round his willing heart.
His body sleeps ; but he himself can hear :
And I will speak to him in measured rhyme ;
For that suits well the dreaming ear of sleep.
True it will fly when waking life succeeds,
As the stars fly when night gives place to day.
But yet some good impression may remain
To woo his erring spirit back to God.

Go thou in memory's deathless power back to thy
    childhood's time

When the soul feels but cannot know the mystery
    of its prime ;
When to the young unfolding sense the meanest
    object brings
A joy unfound in gems of price on diadems of
    kings.
Then 'twas an ever-new delight to wander and
    explore
The wild flowers in the summer woods, the shells
    upon the shore ;
And all fair things that earth could show wore to
    thy wondering eye
The morning glow that never fades from sweet
    eternity.
I see thee in thy father's fields : the sun is on his
    way,
And thou art tumbling with thy mates among the
    new-mown hay ;
And He the Great I Am who sees all things in
    heaven and earth
Looks with an eye of tender love upon thy guile-
    less mirth ;
And 'neath His Spirit's voiceless rule thy being's
    pulses move,
As ocean tides beneath the sway of the gentle
    moon above.

Oh, if all precious things were thine which glad
    the eyes of men,
Would'st thou not gladly give them all to be as
    thou wert then ?
But call upon thy God with tears and break the
    evil spell
That chokes the fountain of thy prayers : and all
    shall yet be well.
And as the suppliant bent to Christ under his
    legal ban,
And rose from leprous misery a healed and happy
    man :
So shalt thou 'scape the deadly doom of sin's
    slow-wasting blight,
And stand thine own true self once more among
    the sons of light.
Yet sigh not for the bliss which passed with
    childhood's years away :
The dew of morning falls but once through the
    long summer day.
But thou in victory over sin shalt taste a joy
    sublime
That fades not under gathering years as fade the
    joys of time :
A joy he cannot hope to know who wastes his
    manhood's power,

Heedless of aught beyond the poor excitement of
    the hour.
Thine be the nobler life of one who, strong in
    heart and limb,
Can endure hardness for the Lord who bore the
    cross for him ;
Who, when he's called upon to tread where
    martyred saints have trod,
Up the steep hill of willing pain to work some
    work for God
In surly winter's beating storm or summer's faint-
    ing heat,
Will still press on although the flint blush neath
    his straining feet.
And as the wandering bird that seeks to gain her
    distant nest
When the fell spirits of the storm howl in their
    wild unrest,
Over the ocean's pathless wastes plyeth her
    weary wing,
Crush thou sloth's puling sickliness by labour's
    healthy swing !
Thus thou, from sin's enslaving wiles enfranchised
    and remanned,
Shalt know the sweetness of God's love, the
    strength of His right hand.

In times of danger and of dread, as well as when
    thy way
Leads through the sheltered vales of peace His
    arm shall be thy stay.
When Nature sleeps in silvery sheen of moonlight
    calm, and when
Leaps the blue levin from the cloud to blast the
    lives of men,
The infant rests in fearless trust upon the
    mother's breast :
So thou on His unchanging love in weal or woe
    shalt rest,
And so from stage to stage of life thine even
    course shalt run,
To God, thy neighbour, and thyself, thy duty
    bravely done :
'Till lapse of years shall bring the time when
    thou shalt soar away
Up to the peaceful vestibule of heaven's eternal day.
For not as the woe-wasted man, when sleep had
    dried his tears,
Wakes back to cold reality from dreams of
    happier years,
Thou from the troublous dream of life, with
    rapture-beaming eye,
Shalt wake to the unfading bliss of great eternity.

JUDITH.

Jael, thy left hand was firm, and heavy the
hammer fell
That sped our proud foe at the heels of his host
to the mirk of the nethermost hell.
When Deborah had gone with the warriors of
God, and the might of her burning
words
Was as wine to the hearts of dispirited men, and
a whetstone to their swords.
Twin stars ye stand in our history's sky in
quenchless light to show
What work for the Lord in troublous times a
woman's weak arm can do.
And last night in a dream methought I was one
of the sons of God who made
Yon cloud-courts ring when His mighty hand the
earth's foundations laid.
I stood on this sea-girt world of ours, and lifted
my wondering eye,
As night's glittering lamps on creation's fourth
day flashed out from the shadowy sky:
Not all at once in a speck of time ; but as through
the sweet summer hours

Star after star on some emerald mead come out
    bright constellations of flowers.
And as on two stars standing lengthways I gazed
    —'twas just ere the vision took flight—
A third star was added, and made with the twain
    a glorious trigon of light.
And I woke as the watch-crowing cock sang the
    dawn that gleamed in the dim eastern
    sky ;
And I knew that the third of those dream-sighted
    stars had read me my destiny.
Great God of my fathers, ensinew my arm for the
    deed
That shall lift up the heads of Thy sons in this
    hour of their need.
The heathen oppressor is waiting to ravin and slay,
As the eagle that poises his wings ere he swoop
    on his prey.
Thou hast dowered Thine handmaid with beauty :
    infuse it with serpentine wile
That shall kill with the honey-sweet charm of a
    treacherous smile.
The hand of a woman shall shatter the horn of
    his trust ;
And the sword of his slayings shall spill his red
    life in the dust.

But to Thee, Lord of hosts, all the honour and
 glory be given
From Thy kingdom on earth to Thy throne in
 the heavens' high heaven!
Upheld by Thine arm, I go forth : by Thy grace
 I aspire
To shine in our history's sky the third in that
 triplet of fire.

LAUGHTER.

Amid sin's harsh discordancies sweet boons of
    sound are given,
Which show that this woe-weary world still links
    itself with heaven.
And such is childhood's ringing laugh, joyous and
    dewy-sweet
As songs of birds at that still hour " when night
    and morning meet."
'Tis the music of the young heart's chords tuned
    by the quick hand of glee,
Without one jarring note to mar its perfect
    harmony.

It falls upon the tired ear as if a seraph-song
Warbled in soothing interlude mid words of
    cruel wrong.
And as the traveller, parched and faint 'neath
    summer's burning ray,
Turns to the cool refreshing spring that gushes
    by the way,
The heart that's weary of the world, by hollow
    forms beguiled,
Drinks in a sweet refreshment from the laughter
    of a child.

But ah, the wingëd joys of youth, how soon they
    fly away,
Like the fair fragile flowers of spring that bloom
    but for a day!
How many a life so blithesome once is as a
    shattered lute
With all its sweet chords rent in twain and all its
    music mute;
And, 'neath the weary bitterness of sorrow's heavy
    chain,
The stricken heart may sadly smile, but never
    laugh again.

And yet the heart, though sorrow-charred, that
    has learned its God to know,
Shall phœnix-like uplift itself from the ashes of
    its woe,
Where all the hell-born brood of sin and death
    shall only be
The echoes of a troubled dream that hath fled
    the memory:
When pain and care and all sad things shall far
    away be hurled,
And great eternity shall solve the riddle of the
    world.

WEARINESS.

Let me sleep, let me sleep!
  My merry mates are gone;
Dark shadows o'er the meadows creep,
  And I am all alone :
              Let me sleep!

Let me sleep, let me sleep!
  The wished-for height is won ;
But oh, the hill-side was so steep
  Under the burning sun :
              Let me sleep!

Let me sleep, let me sleep!
  I cannot stem the flood ;
My weary heart can only weep
  Its woe in tears of blood :
              Let me sleep!

Let me sleep, let me sleep,
  Where spring's sweet daisies grow
Over the slumber still and deep
  Of those who lie below !
              Let me sleep!

FROM BIRTH TO LIFE.

Outbreathed from depths of boundless power
  Which angels long to scan,
With flesh and blood's death-destined dower
  Comes forth the soul of man.
It seems to seek its home afar
  As through its body's eye
It looks up at the little star
  That twinkles in the sky.

With careless step forth fares the boy
  When morn peeps o'er the hill,
And all things bring their draught of joy
  His spirit's cup to fill.
And bright hopes stir within his breast
  Of other things in store
That shall be open to his quest
  When boyhood's days are o'er.

But man a farther stage must reach
  Of hard laborious days
From where pale genius utters speech
  That sets the world agaze

To where beneath the stress of noon
  The rustic sons of toil
Win from the earth her autumn boon
  Of corn and wine and oil.

The old man's head is bent with years ;
  Slow comes his panting breath ;
With faint and faltering steps he nears
  The stony gate of death.
And enters he the grave's cold night,
  Worn with his journey's length ;
But from the crag a youthful sprite
  Upsprings in deathless strength.*

THE END.

* The last of the four stanzas of this poem was
suggested by William Blake's well-known illustration,
" Death's Door."

OGDEN, SMALE AND PETTY, LIMITED, PRINTERS, GT. SAFFRON HILL, LONDON, E.C.

www.ingramcontent.com/pod-product-compliance
Lightning Source LLC
Chambersburg PA
CBHW030025030726
47499CB00008B/3121